JENNIFER ARMSTRONG

# WAN·HU IS·IN THE·STARS

pictures by BARRY ROOT

TAMBOURINE BOOKS · NEW YORK

Printed in Singapore.  The text type is Isbell.  The illustrations were painted in gouache on paper.
Calligraphy by Julian Waters.

Library of Congress Cataloging in Publication Data
Armstrong, Jennifer, 1961–    Wan Hu is in the stars / by Jennifer Armstrong ; illustrated by Barry Root.
— 1st ed.   p. cm. Summary: Absent-minded poet Wan Hu is so curious about the stars that finally, after
several unsuccessful attempts, he finds a way to travel among them. [1. Stars—Fiction.  2. China—Fiction.]
I. Root, Barry, ill.  II. Title. PZ7.A73367Wan 1995  [E]—dc20  94-14815  CIP AC
ISBN 0-688-12457-7 (TR). — ISBN 0-688-12458-5 (LE)
1 3 5 7 9 10 8 6 4 2
First edition

*In memory of my grandmother Mary Katherine Armstrong,*
*who, upon reaching the tender age of sixty-seven,*
*decided to pack her bags and go to Taiwan,*
*and stayed for a couple of years*
*J.M.A.*

*In memory of my aunt Catherine Root*
*B.V.R.*

**O**nce upon a time, in a village near Beijing, there lived a poet named Wan Hu. Wan Hu wandered through his days with an absent mind, often writing his verses with water instead of ink. Wan Hu went about the town dressed in a dark blue robe patterned with lotus, dropping scrolls here, forgetting his ivory signature chop there, and giving pleasant greetings to the pigs.

"Honorable Poet," the gardener said to him one evening. "You are wearing only one shoe."

"Ah, so I am," Wan Hu replied. "I was thinking of the stars, my good gardening friend. I wonder what fine matter they are made of, and what keeps them pinned to the heavens."

The gardener gazed silently at the evening stars and shrugged. Wan Hu gathered his robe around himself and walked off down the pebbled path, one foot bare and one foot shod.

On the following day Wan Hu put a copper rice pot on his head in place of his hat.

"Esteemed Poet," said the gardener. "Permit me to say that you have made a small error in dressing." The gardener indicated Wan Hu's head with a respectful glance, and then bowed.

"Ah," said Wan Hu, taking off the pot and staring at it in surprise. "I was thinking of the stars, my good gardening friend. I wonder how a man might travel among them, and what wisdom he might gain from such a journey."

The gardener gazed silently at the sky and shrugged. Wan Hu gathered his robe around himself and walked off across the wooden footbridge, the copper rice pot twinkling in the sunlight.

On another day soon after, Wan Hu walked out in a steady rain, carrying his folded parasol.

"Illustrious Poet," the gardener said to him. "Perhaps you should open your parasol. You will stay much drier."

"Ah," said Wan Hu, opening it up with relief. "I was thinking of the stars, my good gardening friend. I wonder if, by climbing our mountain, a man might find himself among the heavens. For as you know, our mountain is very high."

The gardener turned to look at the tall mountain. "You will certainly learn the answer if you climb above the mist and clouds," the gardener said to Wan Hu.

"Excellent thought!" Wan Hu exclaimed. And gathering his robe around himself, he set off to climb the mountain.

The people of the village watched him go, and shook their heads.

"Foolish poet," said the silk weaver.

"Scatterbrain," said a landlord.

That night, many people waited for some sign that Wan Hu had reached the stars. But on the following day, Wan Hu returned.

"It is not high enough," he said. "But still, it is my only hope and one desire to be among the stars and learn the secret of their majesty."

His dark blue robe, patterned with lotus, was soiled from his climb, but he folded it around himself as always.

"I wonder," he said to the gardener, "if by harnessing many birds, one might be lifted into the heavens by the power of their wings."

"This may be the answer," the gardener agreed. "The cranes and geese fly very high."

Wan Hu nodded thoughtfully and walked off along the paddy wall.

On the following days, the people in the village saw Wan Hu making silk nooses and waiting for birds to come. He soon had many geese and cranes harnessed in this manner, and tied the ends of their ropes to his hands.

"Lunatic," said the rice merchant.

"Daydreamer," said a lady of wealth.

"Honorable Gardener!" called Wan Hu. "Please scatter the birds and make them fly."

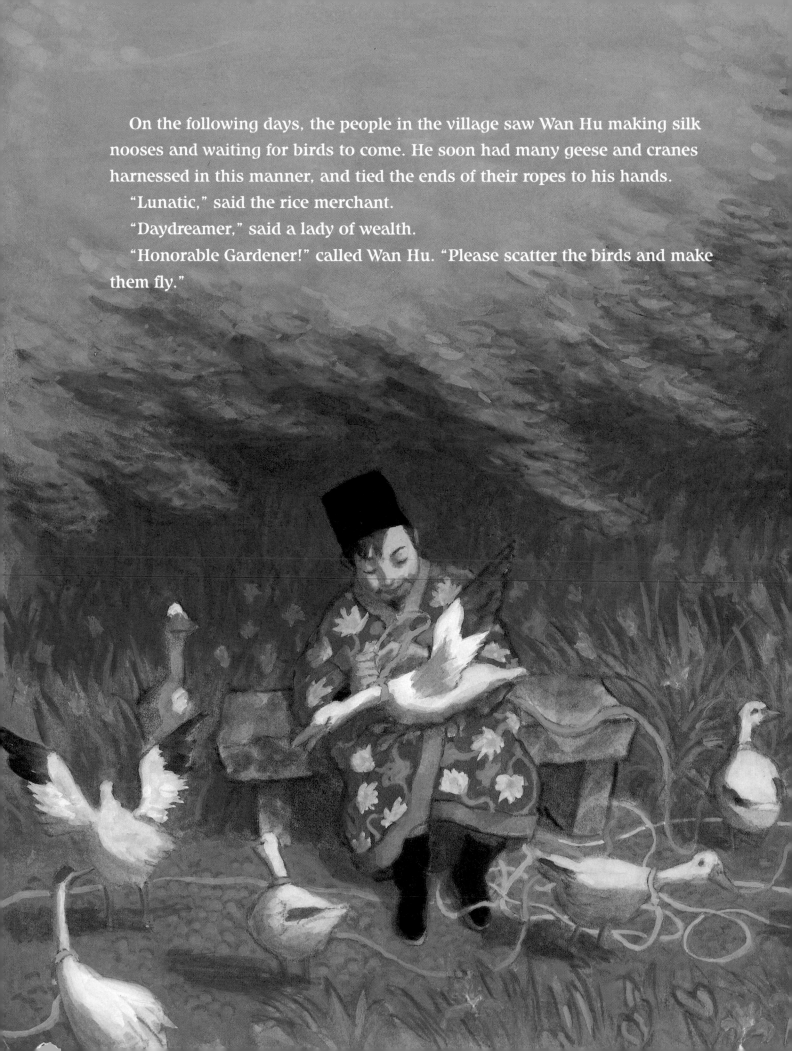

The gardener bowed to Wan Hu and then ran at the flock. The geese and cranes rose in a cloud of beating wings. But the geese went east, and the cranes went west, and all their combined strength was not enough to lift Wan Hu from the ground. He stood like a man with many kites, staring at the sky.

"What nonsense!" said a nanny.

"I knew it would fail!" said a student.

Wan Hu released the birds one by one from their ties, bowed to his neighbors, and walked away.

Soon after, the village celebrated the birthday of the emperor's mother. Boys beat drums, girls waved flags, and the rocket makers lit their splendid fireworks. They burst like flowers and stars over the rice paddies, streaming up into the heavens.

Wan Hu stood on the footbridge, his robe flapping around his legs.

"Ah!" he cried. "This is the answer I have been looking for."

In the morning, Wan Hu went to the rocket makers and bought forty-seven great fireworks from them. While the people of the village watched, he tied the rockets to a bamboo chair.

"You will be burst like the petals of a chrysanthemum in the wind!" cried a neighbor.

"Forget this foolishness. Stay here and revere the ancestors!" cried another.

As evening fell, the crowd gathered around Wan Hu. He gathered up his dark blue robe, patterned with lotus, and sat in his chair.

And then Wan Hu set the forty-seven rockets alight. The crowd pulled back. Wan Hu waved to them all and turned his eyes to the heavens with a blissful smile.

The rockets flashed. The chair and Wan Hu shot up into the sky and soon were lost to sight.

Nobody spoke. A hush of surprise filled the village, and even the pigs stopped grunting.

"He must fall to the earth," whispered the gardener. "I am afraid he will die."

The people searched the night sky for Wan Hu, but there was no sign of him. They waited for days, hoping to hear that the poet had returned to earth at some other village far away.

"He was crazy," said a mason.

"That is what comes of foolish dreams," said the fishmonger.

But some of the people looked at the heavens at night. And there above the village was a sight never seen before. A pattern of stars shaped like a lotus blazed against the dark blue sky over the poet's empty house.

And some believe Wan Hu achieved his only hope and one desire. The gardener is sure that he did.